P9-DCI-684

A Book to Remember

Flyleaf Publishing

Frank The Fish Gets His Wish

Written by
Laura Appleton-Smith

Illustrated by
Preston Neel

Laura Appleton-Smith was born and raised in Vermont and holds a degree in English from Middlebury College. Laura is a primary schoolteacher who has combined her talents in creative writing and her experience in early childhood education to create *Books to Remember*. Laura lives in New Hampshire with her husband Terry. This is her second book from Flyleaf Publishing.

Preston Neel was born in Macon, GA. Greatly inspired by Dr. Seuss, he decided to become an artist at the age of four. Preston's advanced art studies took place at the Academy of Art College San Francisco. Now Preston pursues his career in art with the hope of being an inspiration himself; particularly to children who want to explore their endless bounds.

Text copyright © 1998 Laura Appleton Smith
Illustration copyright © 1998 Preston Neel

All Rights Reserved
Learning Cards may be reproduced for noncommercial purposes only. No other part of this book may be reproduced or transmitted in any form or by any means, electronic, mechanical, photocopying, recording, or otherwise, without the prior written permission from the publisher. For information, contact Flyleaf Publishing.

A Book to Remember™
Published by Flyleaf Publishing
Post Office Box 287, Lyme, NH 03768

For orders or information, contact us at **(800) 449-7006**.
Please visit our website at **www.flyleafpublishing.com**

Second printing, revised
Library of Congress Catalog Card Number: 98-92526
Hard cover ISBN: 0-9658246-1-6
Soft cover ISBN: 0-9658246-6-7

For my parents, Mom and Roy, Dad and Barbara,
who raised me in friendship.
Thank you for your love and support.

LAS

For all children, especially Noli.

PN

Chapter 1: Frank's Big Tank

Once upon a time there was a fish named Frank.

Frank swam in a big glass tank on a shelf in Pat's Pet Shop.

Frank's tank had sand on the bottom.

It had a plant and a pink shell.

It had a pretend ship with a mast and a red flag.

Frank's tank was the biggest and the best tank
in the shop.

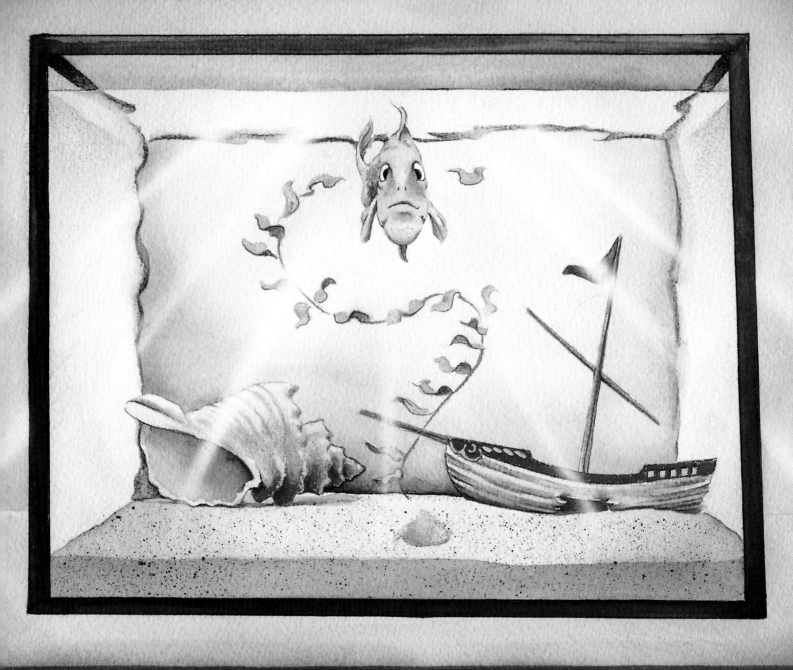

But Frank was sad.

Frank would sit in his pink shell and wish his wish,

"I wish that I had a pal to swim with; to splash and swish and jump with. I would swim the rest of my swims in a dish if I just had a pal to be with."

Each night at dusk, when Pat fed Frank, she would tap the glass on his tank.

"Do not be so sad," she would tell him as she went to the back of the shop to put the cats and dogs and rabbits and frogs and crickets and rats to bed.

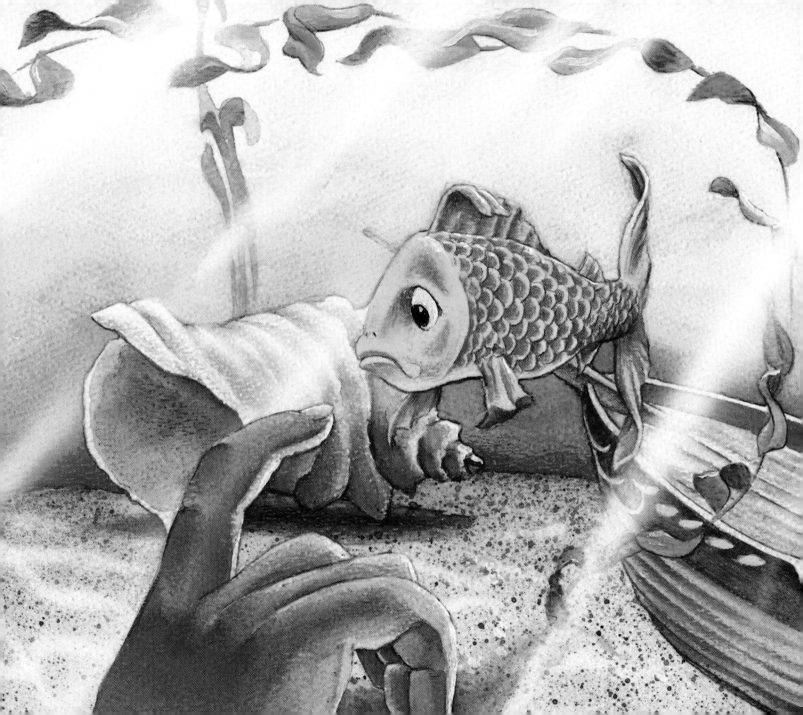

On the shelf, by himself, Frank would sink to the bottom of the tank for his rest.

Chapter 2:
Scruff
the Bad Cat

But one night was different from the rest…

That night, just as Pat went to the back of the shop, Scruff the bad cat slunk in. Scruff crept up on the shelf and got set to fish for Frank.

Scruff put his front leg into the tank, but just as he did the shelf tipped and the tank fell and CRASH it smashed on the pet shop rug.

Bad Scruff ran as fast as a flash back to his bed and hid from Pat.

Pat ran in when the tank crashed and there was her best fish Frank in the slush and bits of glass.

Frank went flip, flop, flap, on the wet pet shop rug.

Pat was so sad. She lifted Frank up in her hands.
What was she to do?

Just then Frank's gills gasped. Pat had to get him
into a tank fast.

In a rush, Pat ran to the back of the shop and dropped Frank into a glass dish.

Frank drifted to the bottom. He was as sad as he had ever been.

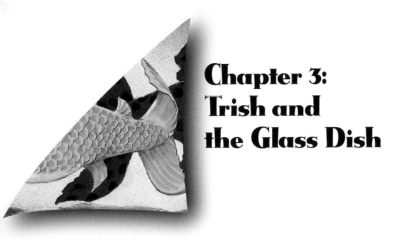

Chapter 3:
Trish and
the Glass Dish

When Frank was strong, he swam a bit. The dish was glass with black rocks on the bottom, but there was no ship, there was no shell, there was no plant.

But then BUMP, Frank bumped into...What was this?

Frank bumped into a fish! She was a red fish with black spots and her fins swished as she swam next to Frank.

The red fish swam fast past the black rocks in the dish. Frank swam fast next to her.

The red fish twisted and Frank twisted.

Frank was so glad. He swam to the top of the dish as fast as a flash. He jumped up and landed with a splash.

The red fish clapped her fins for Frank.

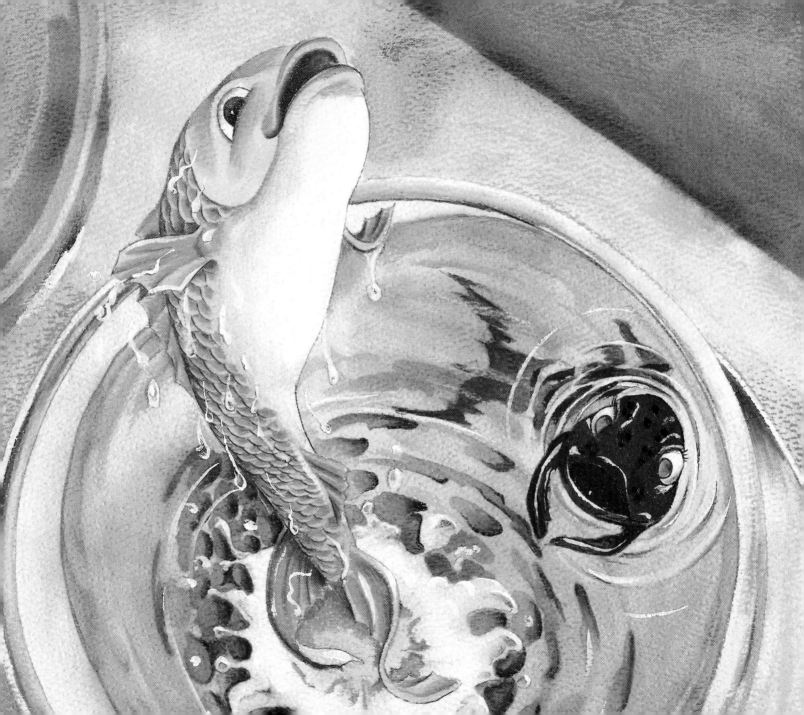

Frank swam back to the red fish.

"My name is Frank," glubbed Frank.

"My name is Trish," glubbed the red fish.

Frank put his fin on Trish's back.

"Trish, I had a wish for a pal to swim with; to splash and swish and jump with. You are my wish, Trish. I am glad I got my wish."

The pals Frank and Trish swam the rest of their swims in the glass dish.

Pat put the glass dish on the shelf where Frank's big tank had sat in the front of the pet shop.

And when kids would visit Pat's Pet Shop,
they would clap for Frank and Trish's tricks
and twists and jumps.

And Frank was not sad, he was as glad
as a fish could be.

Frank the Fish Gets His Wish is decodable with the 26 phonetic alphabet sounds, the "sh" phonogram, and the ability to blend those sounds together.

Puzzle Words are words used in the story that are either irregular or may have sound/spelling correspondences that the reader may not be familiar with.

The **Puzzle Word Review List** contains Puzzle Words that have been introduced in previous books in the *Books to Remember* Series.

The **"sh" words** used in the story are listed for review.

Please Note: If all of the Puzzle Words (sight words) on this page are pre-taught and the reader knows the 26 phonetic alphabet sounds, the "sh" phonogram, and has the ability to blend those sounds together, this book is 100% phonetically decodable.

Puzzle Words:	Puzzle Word Review List:	"sh" words:	"ed" endings:
once upon a	there	**sh**op	clapp**ed**
time	was	**sh**ell	swish**ed**
would	the	**sh**ip	smash**ed**
could	I	**sh**elf	twist**ed**
my	that	fi**sh**	jump**ed**
by	with	wi**sh**	land**ed**
each	to	di**sh**	nam**ed**
one	be	ru**sh**	tipp**ed**
been	night	cra**sh**	crash**ed**
no	when	fla**sh**	bump**ed**
	do	slu**sh**	lift**ed**
	so	swi**sh**	gasp**ed**
	she	Tri**sh**	dropp**ed**
	put	spla**sh**	drift**ed**
	for	sma**sh**	glubb**ed**
	into		
	he		
	ever		
	her		
	this		
	name		
	you		
	their		
	where		
	they		
	of		
	a		
	what		
	then		
	are		

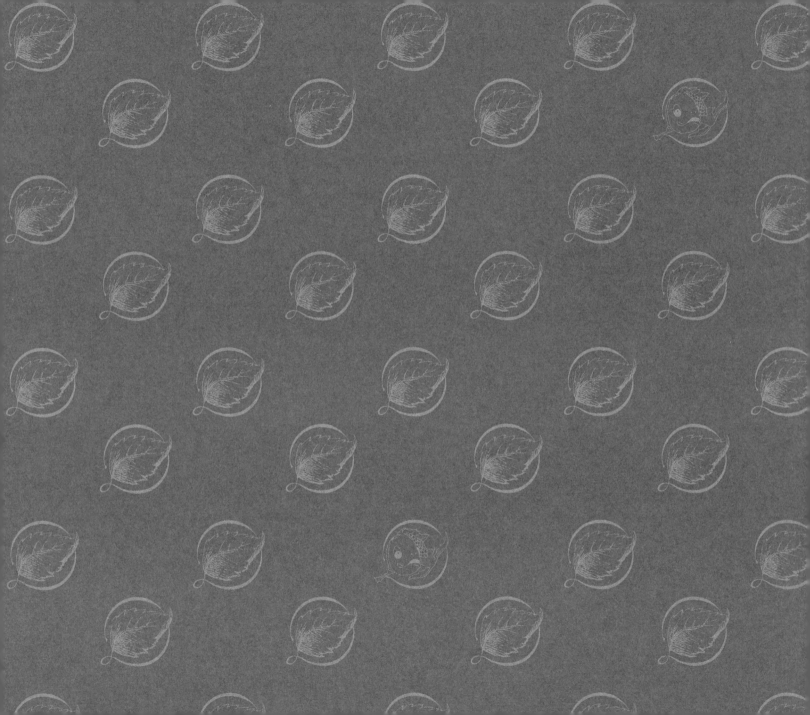